Dancing on the Edge

by

Sharon Jennings

LIBRARY AND ARCHIVES CANADA CATALOGUING IN PUBLICATION

Jennings, Sharon
    Dancing on the edge / Sharon Jennings.

(HIP edge)
ISBN 978-1-897039-27-4

I. Title. II. Series.

PS8569.E563D35 2008   jC813'.54   C2007-906951-7

General editor: Paul Kropp
Text design: Laura Brady
Illustrations drawn by: Catherine Doherty
Cover design: Robert Corrigan

1 2 3 4 5 6 7   08 07 06 05 04 03

Printed and bound in Canada

High Interest Publishing acknowledges the financial support of the
Government of Canada through the Book Publishing Industry
Development Program (BPIDP) for our publishing activities.

When Bonnie Lee crosses Division Street to go to the arts high school, she changes her name and her life. But she has to work hard and take some risks to win respect for her dancing.

CHAPTER ONE

No Turning Back

I stood in the middle of Division Street. One step either way and I could kill myself. If I stepped off the traffic island, I could be hit by a car. I'd be dead in seconds. Or maybe just badly injured. Broken legs. Never able to dance again.

So what? Who cares?

"Are you going to push the button, or what?" Rosa asked.

"Uh-huh." But I kept my hand over the crosswalk button and still didn't move.

Division Street. What genius came up with that name? A six-lane road keeping people like me on our side, down where we belonged. On the south side: poor kids. Public housing losers. Clothing by Goodwill. Kids like me. On the north side: the rich guys. Kids with monster homes and designer clothes.

And now I was supposed to cross Division Street. I was supposed to go to a high school where I didn't belong. Make friends with rich kids. All because . . .

"Bonnie Lee!" yelled Rosa. She shoved my hand and pushed the crosswalk button. Cars came to a stop.

Rosa grabbed me by the arm. She had to haul me across Division Street.

"What the matter with you?"

"Just go on without me," I told her. "I can't do this. I can't go to this arts school. I'm going back home."

I turned and stepped onto the road. I heard tires screech and a horn blare. A man swore out his car window at me.

Rosa dropped her bag and shook me by the shoulders.

"You want I should smack you upside the head?" she demanded.

Every now and then Rosa does her Italian thing. She was starting it now, by pinching both my cheeks.

"What sa matta you? Heh? You *stupeed*?" Rosa put her hands on her hips and glared at me. She looked just like her Nonna when we don't eat all the pasta she makes.

"Oh, Rosa. I'm sorry. It's just. . . . Look, I feel sick. Everything's wrong. We shouldn't be here. We don't belong with these rich kids."

"So we don't have money," Rosa argued. "Big deal."

"But it *is* a big deal," I replied. I didn't have money for dance lessons anymore, and no money for clothes, either. I did a little turn like I was a supermodel. "So how do you like my new back-to-school clothes?" I asked. I was wearing my cousin's hand-me-down jeans. Up on top was a jacket I found at Goodwill. With my luck, some rich kid at City Arts had given it to the clothing drive.

Rosa put her hands on her hips again. "Clothes don't matter. We have talent, Bonnie Lee. It's an art school. We auditioned and got in. We belong as much as anyone else. And besides, you could wear a paper bag and look gorgeous."

I stared at the sidewalk. I had heard all this before. From my mother. From my old teachers. From the neighbors. And from Rosa over and over. So why didn't it sink in? Why was Rosa so excited about City Arts High School? And why was I so afraid?

"Come on, Bonnie Lee. Do it for me, okay? If it doesn't work out, you can quit. You can switch schools. Just give it a try, okay? For me? I don't want to be all on my own."

The truth was, I didn't have the courage either way. I didn't want to go to City Arts. But I didn't have the guts to cross back over Division Street and show up at Edgemont High, either. Too many kids there to laugh at me. Too much history. If I were sixteen, I could just quit school and not worry about it anymore. If only life were that simple.

"It doesn't have to be forever," Rosa said. "Just until I can make some new friends and dump you."

That did it. I finally smiled.

She picked up her bag and linked arms with me.

I've known Rosa since grade one. She came into the classroom hardly able to speak any English and kids made fun of her. But I liked her accent and the cookies she brought for recess. They were made of honey and nuts and she always shared them with me. The other kids called them "foreign" and said "ewwww." Good. More for me. Besides the cookies, Rosa lived around the corner from me. Thanks to her, I finally had someone to walk to school with. Back then she was Rose Angela Maria DiSante.

"In Italy," she told me one day, "everybody calls you by your whole name. It's how people know who you are. Who you belong to. If your name was John Vincent, you'd be Giovanni Vincenzo. Here you're just 'John.' John what? Nobody cares. In Italy, you'd be Bonnie Lee Elizabeth. '*Arrivederci*, Bonnie Lee Elizabeth.' '*Grazia*, Bonnie Lee Elizabeth.' See how it goes? They'd call you by all your names, all the time."

But at the start of grade four, Rose Angela Maria told me she'd changed her name.

"From now on, it's Rosa. That's my new name. I'm tired of everybody telling me I have too many names. And then the teachers just call me Rose. Yuck. No flow."

Suddenly, I stopped walking.

"Now what?" Rosa demanded.

I looked back at Division Street.

Rosa saw me looking.

"Bonnie Lee." She sounded threatening.

"Know when you get a brainwave?" I said. "Like the light bulb suddenly goes on over your head?"

"Not too often," answered Rosa.

"I just had one. And it's amazing. Remember when you became Rosa? Well, guess what? I just got a new name: I'm Lee. Forget the 'Bonnie'. That was my old name. Old life. Gone. Done. Okay?"

"Lee?" she asked, one eyebrow raised.

"Yeah, Lee. I crossed Division Street, so I'm not the same. I'm changed. It's like, it's like . . . " My voice trailed off. I didn't know how to explain what had just happened to me.

"I get it," said Rosa. "You've made a decision that's changed your life. You're not going to Edgemont with all the other kids. You've left behind that old life. So now you're Lee. A new place, a new name. I like it."

"You do?"

"Yeah. Bonnie Lee sounds like a country singer. All twang, twang, twang. But you're not a singer, you're a dancer. Lee sounds like a dancer. Thin. All about lines."

"Yeah, thin. You got that right. No boobs or butt, that's for sure."

"Dancers don't get boobs and butts. That's why I'm not a great dancer. Too curvy. Real dancers get long legs, not like mine."

"Oh, Rosa," I began, but she cut me off.

"Leeeeeee. It sounds like long legs. It's perfect. This is the start of a new life for you, girl."

Yeah, right. Long legs and a new name. But right now, my long legs were shaking

CHAPTER TWO

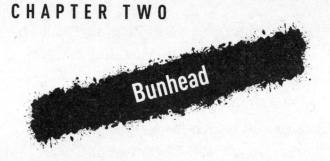

Bunhead

We walked up the hill to City Arts. The parking lot was full of sports cars. The kids were leaning against the walls, wearing clothes to die for. I didn't belong here. Talent means nothing up against real money.

A girl glanced at us, then said something to her friends.

"Hey, bunhead," one of them called. "You're in the wrong place. The trailer park is three blocks south."

I felt my face get hot. Rosa said something rude in Italian.

"Excuse me. Did you say something? I didn't quite hear you," the girl said.

Rosa smiled. "Oh, I'm sorry. I'll speak LOUDER." Then she swore again.

I rolled my eyes and dragged Rosa off. "Oh, Rosa, Rosa. What are you doing to us?!"

"Day one, *cara mia*. You've got to learn to come out swinging."

Then a boy jumped around in front of us. "Your name is *Cara mia*? Cool," he said. He had big brown eyes and thick curly brown hair.

"No, dummy," Rosa answered. "*Cara mia* is Italian. It means 'my dear.' She's Lee. I'm Rosa."

"Gotcha," the guy said. "One of these days I'm going to study Italian."

Rosa laughed. I looked at the guy and pointed to his Fungus World Tour T-shirt. "Did you see them at a concert?"

"Yeah. My dad plays backup when they're on tour."

"Really?"

"Yeah, really," the guy said. "It's no big deal. I mean, Fungus is just a group, like a bunch of other groups."

"Easy for you to say," said Rosa. "So what's your name?"

"Carlos. After Carlos Santana." He shrugged. "My dad's got this thing." Then he smiled and I saw them — dimples. I'm a sucker for dimples.

"So are you in music here?" I wanted to keep this guy talking.

"Yup. I play piano here. But on the outside, I play organ."

"Organ? Like in a church?" Rosa asked. "Great. You can play the 'Wedding March' when we get married."

Carlos laughed and I envied Rosa her easy way with guys. As my mom said, she never took herself seriously. She was open and fun, so people liked to be around her. If Rosa was a flower, I was some kind of a cactus.

"You're in grade nine?" Carlos asked.

"Oh no!" shrieked Rosa. "Does it show?"

Carlos smiled. Dimples again. "You have to be in grade nine or else I would have met you last year. You're both too hot to miss."

I felt something spin inside me, but Rosa just gave Carlos a shove. "You're playing us," she said. "But I don't mind."

"Come on," said Carlos. "I'll show you where the newbies go. There's a welcome thing out back for new guys."

The three of us followed the path to the back of the building. This was easy because someone had painted the pavement yellow. I saw three kids dressed up as Dorothy, the Scarecrow, and the Lion. All of the Oz guys were pointing us along the yellow brick road.

We rounded the corner and saw signs welcoming everyone back to school. Music was playing and a bunch of boys were break dancing. A couple of girls did cartwheels like they were six-year-olds. Everyone was hugging and kissing and looking like they were glad to be back. Except the newbies, of course. All of us stood by ourselves, afraid to join in. Afraid the music would suddenly stop and everyone would look at us and point.

I hugged my bag to my chest like it was the teddy bear I'd left at home on my bed. Rosa nudged me. "This isn't what I expected."

I had to say it. "Well, Toto, we're not in Kansas anymore."

But I knew what she meant. It didn't look like *all* the kids had attitude. And only *some* were wearing designer clothes. Most were wearing the weirdest stuff, like something they got out of Mr. Dressup's tickle trunk. And some of them looked like they'd cut their own hair and then put on food coloring.

Carlos waved to some guy and said he'd see us around. Then a girl came over to us. She was very short and her hair was in dreadlocks. I thought I'd seen her before, but I didn't know where.

"You're Bonnie Lee, right?" she asked. "I've seen

you at lots of competitions. You win everything. I'm Nicole."

"Oh yeah! Hi. But my name is Lee, now. Forget the Bonnie."

Nicole nodded her head. "Cool. Are you still at the same dance studio?"

I shook my head. "I'm not dancing this year. I . . . uh . . . needed a break. And I wanted to come here," I lied. The truth was worse — that I had to drop out when my dad stopped sending support money.

"You've quit?! I don't believe it! You were fabulous! How could you quit?"

Maybe she saw the look on my face.

"Sorry. None of my business, right?" said Nicole.

"It's okay," I said. "It's just . . . stuff. You know."

Nicole nodded. Maybe she did understand. But I looked at her designer jeans and running shoes and I doubted it. Rich kids never really get it.

"This is Rosa. She's in dance, too."

"You're gonna love it," said Nicole. "I had a blast last year."

Nicole was in grade ten. So she had always been a level ahead of me at competitions. That's why I didn't remember her.

She went on. "Some kids think they're God's gift. But most are nice." She laughed. "The boys are great. Not too many of them, and some are gay, so some of the girls get a little weird. Some real bitchy stuff about who gets a date. And most of the divas are in dance. Tough for us."

She turned to the driveway. "Speak of the devil."

A BMW two-seater pulled up to the curb. A gorgeous girl got out. She was tall with long blonde hair. But the outfit was over the top — a cream Aritzia track suit. Big bucks. Then I saw the matching Prada sandals and purse. Real big bucks.

"Looks like Victoria came back after all," Nicole said. "Last year she said she was going to New York, but I guess it didn't work out."

"Victoria," I asked.

"We call her Queen Victoria. She thinks she's really something."

"She looks it," said Rosa.

"Oh, she is. And she knows it. She's been the teacher's pet for two years, if not forever. I'd keep out of her way if I were you."

The bell rang and the crowd started to move inside.

We were told where to pick up our schedules, and we headed to home room. All the classes were a mix of dancers, musicians, theater kids and artists.

Our teacher seemed nice, pretty laid back. He explained some rules and told us to come to him for advice. Then he said we'd have a shortened first day. One hour for each of our four classes. Full day tomorrow.

The bell rang and we were off to ballet. The newbies got stuck with dance first period every day, whether our bodies were still asleep or not.

We went straight to the change room. Our teacher was waiting for us when we came out. She was shorter than me and really, really thin. Her black hair was pulled back in a very tight bun. She was leaning on a cane, but she looked like a real ballerina.

"I am Madame Wolfson," she said. "Every day you must wear correct ballet attire. Do you understand? Plain black body suits and pink tights. I will not tolerate junk clothing. I shall send you to the office. Please make sure your hair is in a bun." She grabbed a girl's pony tail. "What's this?" she demanded. "Get rid of it. Now."

The girl pulled her hair into a quick bun.

Madame Wolfson wasn't finished. "Regular school starts at 9:00. But dance starts at 8:45. I expect you here, properly dressed, hair done and at the barre warming up. Am I clear?"

Some of us nodded and said sure, yeah, right.

Madame Wolfson smacked her cane on the barre.

"Were you raised in a barn? It is 'Yes, Madame Wolfson.' Proper dress and proper behavior. This is a ballet class, not a nightclub. Do you understand?"

"Yes, Madame Wolfson," we all answered.

Then Madame Wolfson spun around and pointed at me. "You," she said, "come here. What is your name?"

"Lee," I answered. I didn't even think about it. My name really was Lee, now.

"Perfect," she said, touching my hair. "You see, girls. This is what a bun should look like."

After ten years, I could do a ballet bun in my sleep. Not one hair out of place. I mean, it isn't like I solved world hunger or anything, but I could fix my hair. I made a face and smiled at the other girls. A couple smiled back at me, but a few rolled their eyes. Pony-tail girl just glared.

"Girls, find a place at the barre. Let us begin."

The exercises were basic, the stuff you learn when you're six. I hadn't danced all summer, not since my mom broke the news. So, of course, I was a bit stiff, but then I heard the music, *felt* the music, and I couldn't have stopped my body from moving if I had tried.

Madame Wolfson was right at my side. "Lovely

turnout. Lovely. Be careful. Don't lock your knees. That's it. Lovely. Girls. Look at Lee's feet. See how she stretches them? Beautiful." And she moved on.

I caught the eye of pony-tail girl. What's that expression? If looks could kill? If they could, I'd be dead right this minute.

A bell rang and we raced to change. Madame Wolfson called out, "I expect to see all of you at the tryout for our dance company." It wasn't a question. "Next Monday at 2:30."

"You're coming with me," I whispered to Rosa.

"Of course I am. If I get into the school company, I'll quit my other lessons. A school group will be way more fun."

I looked at my schedule. "I have math now."

"English. See you later." Rosa moved off down the hall.

I picked up my bag and turned around. Pony-tail girl was blocking my way. She glared at me. "I guess the Wolf's found her teacher's pet for the year. *Perfect. Lovely. Beautiful.* Don't you just want to gag?"

I watched her leave the change room. I looked at her clothes, the jewelry, the purse and shoes. She hadn't crossed Division Street to come to City Arts. She belonged here.

CHAPTER THREE

Audition

The audition was packed. Every dancer at City Arts wanted to be in DansCool. It was the school dance company — DansCool. Get it? Dance School. Dance Cool.

If you got in, you stayed after school for rehearsals and put on several shows a year. Some shows were just for our own students, but sometimes the company traveled to all-school competitions or put on shows all over the city.

"Well, it's not what you're used to," Rosa told me.

"But at least you're still dancing, and in front of a real audience. No judges. No marks."

"No trophies," I added.

Rosa smiled. She knew about my trophies. I had smashed all of them the day my mom said she couldn't afford dance lessons. Childish? Yeah, but it felt good.

I looked around at all the kids. I saw some newbies, but most kids were from the older grades. The newbies looked nervous, like me. DansCool wasn't for newbies.

I started feeling sick, just like I used to get at competitions. First my stomach starts knotting up, then I feel like I'm going to faint. Rosa took one look at me and knew.

"Stop it, Lee. You'll be great. Just remember you *like* dancing. You don't *have* to be here. You *want* to be here."

I nodded. I did want to be here. I had nothing else anymore. I had to get into DansCool. It wasn't about being the best or beating other dancers. It really was about the dance. Just dancing. Just feeling the music inside of me and forgetting about the rest of the world.

Then I remembered what my teacher said to me last year. I was about to go onstage, and I thought I was going to pass out. My teacher grabbed my arm and said, "I don't want you to compete." I thought he meant not to go onstage. I thought he'd changed his mind about me, but that wasn't it. "I just want you to *dance*. Don't *compete*." And then relief flooded my body. I didn't care about winning. I only cared about the dance.

The memory made me feel better. I could do this. I smiled at Rosa. Then pony tail girl walked by us. She looked us up and down and said something to another girl. The two of them laughed.

"Ugh," said Rosa. "That's Julie. She's in two of my classes. A real nose-in-the-air type, if you know what I mean."

Then Madame Wolfson tapped her cane on the floor.

"We have a very large group to audition," she began. "I wish you could all be in DansCool, but of course that is not possible."

We all knew the odds. There were twelve dancers in DansCool. But there must have been fifty of us in the gym. One chance in four, at best.

"Please stop talking and listen carefully. First, you will do across the floor exercises. Then you will perform combinations in groups. I will be looking for technique *and* performance. And remember to smile."

Then some other teacher put on music and led us into the warm-up. Kids pushed to get up to the front, to be seen. I knew all about these kinds of kids. I'd met lots of them at dance workshops. They're the type that stand at the front, wanting all the attention. They wear tight little booty shorts and crop tops to show off their abs. And when the teacher asks the ones at the front to switch places with the dancers at the back, they never move. They're just so sure the world is all about them.

So now, I stayed at the back. It wasn't crowded, but this girl hit me in the chest with her arm. Then another girl whacked me in the back of the head with her hand. I turned quick to look at them. They pretended not to notice. It's only the warm-up and these guys are out for blood.

After ten minutes, Madame Wolfson called for the first year kids to line up.

Rosa and I moved into place. Rosa squeezed my hand.

It was easy stuff. First we did traveling *pas de bourées* across the floor. On our second time across, we did two jettes and a fan kick. Then we did step, step, step, kick, step, step, step, kick. Some kids didn't know to alternate legs. Some seemed to forget they even had arms. At last we did a double pirouette. That was a joke. Only a handful of kids could even turn.

As soon as I finished my lines, I watched the other dancers. I couldn't believe how bad most of them were. Dancers? As if! How did they get into this school? Half of them didn't even point their toes. Only Nicole and one other girl bothered to stretch their feet. And some of those who looked good were just cheating. You tilt your hip to get your leg higher and the audience loves it. But your ballet teacher will chew you out afterwards. I had to admit that some of the kids were good dancers, but they had style, not much technique. I caught a look at myself in the mirror. My face sure showed what I was thinking.

Now it was the grade elevens' turn. Victoria strutted out into place and raised her chin high. I suddenly got why they called her Queen Victoria. I had to admit she had a beautiful body. Really long legs and gorgeous face. She was first in line and she knew that everyone was watching her. And she was good. Not great, her style was what my old teacher called "cheesy." And her technique needed work. But, boy, she could really sell it.

I turned to Rosa. I stuck my finger down my throat and pretended to be sick. A couple of kids

around me saw and laughed. Madame Wolfson saw
me and frowned. Oops.

And so it went on. Kids with not much going for
them, sweating and smiling and giving it all they
had. A couple of guys, too. One was pretty good. A
couple of others had a lot of attitude but needed
work. I shook my head. This was going to be easy.
A cinch.

Madame Wolfson read from a list. "These students
have made the first cut." She read out thirty names.
I was on it, of course, and I nodded when she called
my name. But other kids! They cheered and jumped
up and down. A couple of kids started to cry. Even
Rosa punched her fist in the air when her name was
read out.

The kids who didn't make it went home. They
looked beaten up, or worse. Beaten up inside. I
know, because I've been there.

"I wouldn't have chosen half these kids," I said to
Rosa. Madame Wolfson was walking by and gave me
a look.

"Shut up!" hissed Rosa.

So now thirty of us danced together in our lines across the floor. Same easy stuff, no hard lines. Nothing like what I got at my old company. But some of these kids were really sweating, pushing to do basics that were so easy for me.

Rosa finished her jette line and wiped her face with a towel. "Isn't this great? I love this! I have to get into DansCool!"

"Of course you will. Haven't you been watching? The rest of these guys are hopeless."

It was my turn. I was right behind Queen Victoria, so I couldn't resist. I added in a couple of tricks to the basic drill. A couple of kids cheered. Victoria turned quickly to see what was going on. I finished with a triple pirouette and said "ta dah" just for laughs. Victoria's face went hard as I finished.

Then Madame Wolfson pounded her cane. "Lee, I asked for one pirouette, not a triple."

I was stunned. "Yes, but I can do ... "

"I do not really care what you *think* you can do,"

interrupted Madame Wolfson. "I asked for a single pirouette because that shows me your control."

Oh, as if she couldn't see my control a mile away. I rolled my eyes.

Madame Wolfson nodded to Victoria. "Please show Lee a *single* pirouette."

Victoria went to the center of the floor. Her preparation was perfect and so was her pirouette.

"Thank you, my dear." Madame Wolfson looked over at me.

"Do you want me to do a pirouette again?"

"No, thank you. We've wasted enough time."

I couldn't believe this. Why was she picking on me? No wonder her nickname was the Wolf.

I watched some of the other dancers do their audition. I didn't notice Victoria standing beside me until she spoke.

"Lee?" Victoria whispered. She smiled really sweetly and put her hand on my arm. Her nails dug into my skin. "Don't ever upstage me again. Do you understand? Don't. Not ever. Or you *will* be sorry."

She dropped my arm and walked away.

I stared at her back, my heart pounding. I saw Julie smirking at me and I turned around, rubbing my arm.

Nicole came over. "I told you. I told you to keep out of her way."

"Oh this is stupid!" I exclaimed. "Who does she think she is?"

Nicole shrugged. "She's the Queen. She's perfect. Everybody knows that. Everyone leaves her alone. But now you're a threat. I saw her watching you when you danced. She knows you're good, Lee. If you get in, I'm thinking we're in for an awesome catfight this year."

Madame Wolfson clapped her hands. Then she explained the next part.

"If you attend a real audition, dancers, you have only minutes to learn a routine. And then only seconds to impress whomever will hire you. So please pay attention." Then she explained what she wanted us to do. She watched as we marked our way through the steps.

We had two minutes of practice before we performed. That's tough, real tough. Some kids were AWFUL! I went up with my group, and we had no trouble at all. I couldn't resist a little yawn at the end of the piece.

And then the moment all of us were waiting for. Thirty people in the room. Twelve would make DansCool. Madame Wolfson called out Rosa's name first and Rosa let out a huge squeal. Then Madame Wolfson read Nicole's, Victoria's and Julie's names. She read out seven other names, including the two boys who had shown up. Natch. Eleven names. One name to go.

I looked at Rosa, holding my breath. Surely I was number twelve.

But Madame Wolfson didn't call out my name. "Azama," she said, "you complete the company."

Madame Wolfson took off her glasses. She was finished. She hadn't called my name.

CHAPTER FOUR

Confession

"Idiot!" Rosa shouted at me. She pushed me in the chest with both hands. "Stupid idiot! Why did you have to do that?!"

"Do what?" I shouted back. "Dance better than everyone else?"

Rosa swung out of the change room and smashed the door. I stood in the empty room for a minute, then ran after her.

"What did I do? What did I do?" I yelled.

Rosa turned around and glared at me. "I don't

know what *you* did. Because that wasn't *you* at the audition. That was someone I didn't know. That person, that *stranger,* was just as bitchy as the girls you hate."

"I don't know what you're talking about."

"Oh yes you do. You just had to show off, didn't you? You had to make it so obvious that you're better than everyone else, didn't you? And now what? I get to be in DansCool without you. Just great. We came here together, moron. We wanted to dance *together*. But you've blown it."

Rosa turned and went outside.

I stood in the hallway shaking. How dare she? How *dare* Rosa say that? I didn't blow anything. Stupid Madame Wolfson blew it. I banged my fist on a locker.

"Ouch! What did my locker ever do to you?"

It was Carlos. I had seen him around the school lots since last week. He was always with a different girl.

I turned away.

Carlos reached for my hand. "What gives?"

I felt the tingle, just like I was in some stupid romance novel.

"Nothing. It's personal." I tried to leave again but he stood in front of me.

"Come on, *cara mia*. You can tell me. I promise I won't tell a soul. Cross my heart and hope to die." Then he sat down right in front of me, his chin in his hands.

I had to smile. He sounded like a little kid. He looked like a little kid.

"Hey! There's a smile. Now start talking." He patted the floor.

"Here?"

"Sure. No one's around."

Well, why not? My best friend took off on me, and I didn't feel like going home. So I slid down a locker onto the floor.

"You look awful. Who died?" Carlos asked.

"I did." I blinked my eyes, but I couldn't help it. I started to cry.

"Wow. Come on, tell me. This has to be good."

"I blew the audition for DansCool."

"No way. I've heard people talking all week about how great you are."

"Well, Madame Wolfson doesn't think so."

"But she does," Carlos replied. "I've heard you're her new teacher's pet. And I've heard Victoria hates you."

"How do you know so much?"

"Easy. Word gets around."

I pulled back from him. "Is that all this is to you? Gossip?"

I started to stand up, but Carlos pulled me down. "Not gossip. I really like you. I've been thinking about you all week."

I looked at Carlos. I mean, I really looked at him. Could I trust him? Or was he just a player?

"Trying to see into my soul?" Carlos asked.

I laughed. "Do you have one?"

He reached out and touched my lips. "You're smiling. You're gorgeous when you smile." Then he smiled too and there were those great dimples.

"Tell me what happened," Carlos said, and he reached for my hand.

"I . . . I'm not sure. My best friend said it wasn't me in there. And . . . and I guess she was right. I was so worried about not making it and then I . . . well . . . when I saw the level of dancing I was so relieved. And then I started showing off." I suddenly remembered the "ta dah" and the little yawn and I felt really embarrassed. I felt myself going all red. And, oh great, the water works started up again. I pulled a tissue from my bag.

"But you dance in a company, don't you?" Carlos asked. "You don't need DansCool, right?"

I shook my head. "Wrong. I used to dance in a company. But my mom can't afford it anymore."

Carlos didn't say anything. He gave my hand a squeeze.

"One day my dad went to work and he didn't come home," I told him. "He used to send us some money, but then he stopped. My mom couldn't track him down. She struggled all last year with the bills, but my dance class had to go. So if I don't dance here, I don't dance at all."

Carlos didn't answer. He sat there frowning. And then he said, "Why don't you go talk to the Wolf? Tell her all this stuff."

I shook my head. "There's no way I could do that. I can hardly face her in class now." I suddenly realized what I was saying. "I guess I'm going to switch schools. Go to Edgemont after all. It's where I really belong."

"So you'd give up this easy?" Carlos demanded. He stared hard at me. "If dance means so much to you, fight for it. Go talk to Madame Wolfson. Maybe she'll give you a second chance," Carlos urged.

I knew I would never do that. Never. But I smiled at Carlos and said, "Maybe. I'll think about it." I stood up to go.

"Don't go yet," Carlos said. "I want you to hear something." He grabbed my hand and ran down the hall, pulling me with him.

He stopped at the door marked "Music Room." We went inside and I looked around at all of the instruments. Carlos went over to a piano and started playing. He pounded on the keys — really pounded. I knew the piece. I mean everyone knows that part of Beethoven's Fifth Symphony. You don't have to study music, just watch Saturday morning cartoons. TA TA TA TAAAA. TA TA TA TAAAA.

Carlos swung around. "Isn't that perfect? I mean isn't that just how you feel inside?" He turned back to the piano and kept playing. I closed my eyes and listened.

"See?" said Carlos. "You know what Shakespeare said — 'music to soothe the savage beast.'"

I nodded. Not about the Shakespeare thing, but about music. "That's why I dance," I told him. "I listen to the music and try to figure out what it's telling me. And then I try to tell a story through movement."

Carlos was about to say something and then he stopped. He was looking at somebody behind me.

"Then it is truly a shame you did not do that at your DansCool audition."

The voice cut right through me. I spun around.

Madame Wolfson was behind me.

CHAPTER FIVE

I thought I was going to faint. I think Carlos stopped playing but I couldn't hear anything, anyway. My ears were pounding. I knew I was going all red and I knew I was going to cry. I put out a hand for a chair and sat down.

Madame Wolfson turned to Carlos. "You play beautifully. The school is lucky to have you." Then she looked at me. "The school should have been lucky to have you, too, Lee. But sometimes, students do not fit in the way we expect."

I closed my eyes. Go away, I wanted to tell her. Just go away. Then I heard the door open and close. She left, thank God! I opened my eyes. I was alone with Madame Wolfson. Carlos had deserted me. I slunk down in my seat.

Madame Wolfson sat down across from me, her back ramrod straight. "I wanted you in my company very badly. But your attitude is all wrong. You made it very clear that you're better than those other girls. Did you think that I do not know that? I saw your talent the first minute on the first morning in class. You have a gift, a very special gift. A teacher waits years for someone like you. But attitude counts for so much. The students I chose this afternoon all want to be there. They will fight and work hard for everything they get. They have passion! You made it clear you were bored. I cannot have a bored dancer in my company."

She finally stopped talking. I didn't look at her. She waited, expecting me to say something. "I understand," I managed to whisper. "I'm switching schools. I'll transfer to Edgemont. It doesn't matter."

"I am sorry to hear that. I would still like to have you in my class. Please think it over. It would mean very much to me to be your teacher."

I felt the tears flow down my face. Madame Wolfson handed me a tissue. I took it and blew my nose. Too hard. It made a funny noise and I let out a sort of laugh sob. And then I broke down.

"I'm sorry, Madame Wolfson. I'm so sorry. I didn't mean to . . . to act like that. That's not me. It isn't me. Rosa is right. I wanted to be in DansCool so bad. I really did. And now . . . and now I don't know what I'm going to do."

I told her about my dad and about leaving my old studio. I told her about being afraid to come to this school, about not fitting in. I even told her about changing my name. I went on and on. Once I started talking, I didn't think I could stop. "I was scared and worried and when I saw the others dance I knew I'd get in the company and so I showed off and I wanted to put Queen — I mean Victoria in her place and even my best friend is disgusted with me and . . ."

"Child," Madame Wolfson touched my face, "I understand. You have been under a huge strain. I cannot imagine how you felt giving up dance lessons. But I think that you must stay at this school. You have crossed Division Street. You are here now with a new name and a new set of problems. That is a wonderful story. Please stay with us and be my student. I am sorry that I cannot give you a place in the company, but I do wish to work with you. I do think that will be best for you."

Madame Wolfson leaned on her cane and stood up. "So I will see you tomorrow at 8.45." I nodded. Then I remembered. "Yes, Madame Wolfson," I said.

I watched her leave the room. I didn't know if she would see me tomorrow or not. I had to figure this out. Where else would I dance if not here? But how could I face the other dancers? Wouldn't the other kids make fun of me? Julie and Victoria would never stop. But where would I dance? Where would

I dance? I shook my head as if that would straighten things out. Then I picked up my knapsack and opened the door.

"Finally!" said Carlos. "I didn't want to bother you, but what took you so long? The Wolf left ten minutes ago."

I looked at him. "Let me guess. You were just listening."

"Every word! Wow! She really likes you."

"Not enough to put me in the company," I answered.

"Well, it wouldn't look good, would it? But I bet she'll find something for you to do. I mean, you're 'a gift.'"

I hit him with my knapsack. He grabbed it and laughed at me. I smiled up at him and felt suddenly really good. I didn't know why. Things couldn't be worse, but somehow I felt a little bit better. "I've got to get going," I said.

"I'll go with you."

We went outside and walked down the hill. I

took in a deep breath of fresh air. I could smell the flowers from someone's garden.

"Where do you live?" I asked.

"Up Pinecrest."

It figured. His dad toured with Fungus. They must be rolling in money. Carlos sure looked it. His hair was always perfect. He wore expensive cologne. And his scruffy leather jacket was designed that way and must have cost a fortune. And then there were his hands. Long, long fingers and manicured nails. All the boys I knew had grungy nails and bit them.

"You have nice hands," I blurted out.

Carlos held them up. "Can't touch the keyboard with dirty fingers." He smiled and reached out a hand to my face. With one finger he traced my cheekbone. "And I'd only touch you with clean fingers, if you let me."

I stopped walking and looked at him. I had to ask. "Are you always like this with girls? I mean, are you just . . . " I didn't know how to finish without sounding stupid.

"Playing with you?" he asked. He moved his body in closer to mine. "Sure. I play with all the pretty girls. But I think with you it's different. I think maybe you're special."

I swallowed and looked away from him. I had been looking out for him all week, trying to see him and what he was doing. I had thought about him every night, wondering what it would be like to be with him. And now, here he was, and I was suddenly really nervous. I moved away from him and started walking.

"So you think I should stay here? Stay at City Arts?" I asked.

"I think you have to stay here," he answered. "You can work out all your stuff. Figure out who you are. And then I can see you every day."

We reached the street. "I guess we part here," I said. "I live south of Division, you know, the poor part of town."

Carlos rubbed two fingers together. "World's smallest violin. Cause you're feeling so sorry for yourself. See? You have to stay at this school. It doesn't matter about money here."

"Easy for you to say."

"Yeah, okay, I live in a big house. Big deal. My mom left my dad years ago when she found out he was a daddy to lots of other children scattered around the world. I stayed with my dad because of my music. My sisters live with my mom in Vancouver. I hardly ever see my dad because he travels so much. Mostly I eat dinner with the house-keeper. Happy?"

I raised my hand and rubbed two fingers together. "Hey! I'm a musician too!"

Carlos smiled and I laughed. And then I don't know where the question came from, but I suddenly asked, "Do you have a girlfriend now?"

Carlos looked at me. "I think so."

Then he leaned down and kissed me. Just a light, little kiss on the lips. A brush. Nothing more.

Still, I felt something twist inside me.

CHAPTER SIX

A Second Chance

It was pretty hard telling my mom about DansCool. The look on her face made me feel really awful all over again.

"Oh Bonnie Lee! What happened?" My mom looked so upset, not angry. So I told her everything. I actually got through the whole thing without crying. But my mom cried. "Nothing's working for you, is it, baby?"

Well, something was working for me, but I didn't tell her about *that*. One day I'd tell her about Carlos, but I wanted it to be my secret for a while.

"You know, I had this summer job once. It was great. They really loved me, so I assumed they'd hire me back the next summer. And they would have, but I kept putting off calling them so they hired someone else. When I finally called them, I was so sure I had the job. I didn't. I thought I was going to die. I was so embarrassed and I felt so stupid. The worst part was I really wanted to work there." Then my mom sighed and hugged me. "Well, live and learn, baby. What doesn't kill you makes you stronger." That's my mom. Just a nice, nice person. I think I hated my dad a bit more after that.

That's when I finally found the nerve to tell my mom about my name change. All week long I had been putting it off. I felt sick every time she called me Bonnie Lee. But now, I blurted out the truth. "Mom, you know how I'm named Bonnie Lee for dad's mom and your mom right?" She nodded, and I told her.

Mom took it well. She even found it funny. "Lee.

I like that. And I never did like my nosy mother-in-law. You go for it, baby!"

Next, I had to apologize to Rosa. Right after supper I walked over to her house. I picked a few flowers out of someone's garden on the way and held them out to Rosa.

"I'm sorry. You were right. I am a stupid idiot."

Rosa buried her face in the flowers. "Nice. Remind me to thank Mrs. Stewart for her roses." Then she held out her arms and I moved in for her hug. Lots of hugs tonight. I told Rosa what happened after she left me. And of course I told *her* about Carlos.

"You brazen hussy!" Rosa cried. "You stole my boyfriend! I told you I was going to marry him. I told *him* I was going to marry him! How dare he?!" Then she fell down laughing. "Well, at least one of us got him."

"It was just a kiss, Rosa. I mean, I really like him, but . . ."

"But what?" she demanded.

"But . . . well, I see him all the time with other girls. It's just a feeling, that's all," I finished.

"So keep it cool. You don't have to fall all over him right away. You can let him see you with other boys," she suggested. "Make him wonder a bit, too."

I nodded, and then I suddenly realized that I had made up my mind. I was going to stay at City Arts after all.

"I thought about switching schools," I confessed to Rosa. "But now I'm not. And *not* because of Carlos."

Rosa raised her eyebrows. "Yeah, right," she said.

"Well, maybe a bit because of Carlos. Because of what he said. And because of what Madame Wolfson said. I've got to stay there and work things out. I don't want to cross back over Division. I don't want to be Bonnie Lee anymore."

So I showed up the next morning at 8:45, pink tights, black leotard, hair in a bun. All the other kids went quiet when I walked into the change room. That's how I knew they'd been talking about me.

With Julie's help, of course. So by now, I guessed everybody knew I didn't make the company.

I felt so stupid. All last week things looked like they might work out. Now, I was an outcast. The others looked away from me. But not Julie. "Boy, Lee, you really blew it last night, didn't you?" In a very loud voice. "I mean, you were so . . . so . . . now what was the word? Oh I remember, so *perfect* in class. I mean, what happened?" She sounded like she was being all concerned about me.

"Oh, shut up, Julie," said a girl I didn't know. "Leave her alone. Hey! How many of us didn't make DansCool? Show of hands!"

Only Julie and Rosa didn't put up their hands. "See," said the girl, waving her hand. "You're in great company, Lee. Don't worry about it."

I smiled at her. I took my place at the barre and danced the best I could. Madame Wolfson didn't pay any special attention to me that day or for the rest of the week. Maybe she knew it would make things worse for me.

But Julie didn't let things go. Every day in dance class she had something more to say to me. Things like, "Why, isn't your turnout *lovely*." Or, "My, what a *beautiful* bun!" I wanted to smack her face. I wanted to push her down and rip her designer clothes off her body.

I didn't.

At the end of the week, she asked, "By the way, where did you get your dance bag? It's so unique. Goodwill?"

I felt the anger rise up again. Of course, her bag was brand new Lululemon. Mine was years old nothing. But suddenly something clicked inside of me. I said, "Thank you. I got it second-hand at the Salvation Army. I really like it. It's vintage." And I smiled at her like she was my best friend. "I'll take you to the Sally Ann if you want. Vintage is so hot right now."

It worked. She didn't know what to do. She sort of half smiled back and walked away.

"You are learning," said Madame Wolfson behind

me. "Your story is growing and taking shape."

What on earth did she mean by that? What story? She said something about that last week, too. About crossing Division Street being my story. I walked down the hall trying to figure this out and, of course, I kept looking for Carlos. Every day I hoped to bump into him. But trying to look cool, if I did. And if I saw him, he'd hurry over and put his arm around me.

Thank goodness math was next. I could forget about everything during math class. Rosa doesn't get it but to me it's so easy. There are rules and you are either right or wrong. Not like English, where everybody has a different opinion about one piece of writing. We argued about it at lunch.

"How can you be so stupid in English?" Rosa demanded. "You interpret music, don't you? You tell a story with movement and music. With English someone tells a story using words. Same thing. And how can you be good in math? What story can you tell with numbers?"

"But dance is like math," I answered. "It's logical. There's rules. And it's all done to music and counts and rhythm."

Rosa shook her head. "You should have a talk with Einstein." Then she suddenly jumped up and waved her hands. I looked behind me. She was waving to Carlos. I felt myself flushing. Not cool. I grabbed my water bottle and took a big gulp to hide my face.

"Hello, Casanova," said Rosa.

"Okay. I'll bite. Why am I a Casanova?"

Rosa rolled her eyes. "First day of school, I told you I wanted to marry you. And as soon as my back is turned, you fall for my best friend. Wait a minute. You're not a player. You're a *ciuco*."

"What's a *choocho*?" asked Carlos.

"*Ciuco* is a donkey, an ass," Rosa explained.

"An ass? Just for that, I won't tell you who likes you," he replied.

Rosa put her arm around him. "Don't tease me, *bello*. And *bello* means beautiful, by the way."

Carlos smiled. "The grade ten guys always check out the newbie dancers. Hope to get a head start on making it with someone with a great bod." He ran his fingers down my back, stopping his hand on my waist. There was that twisting feeling again. I settled back in my chair, pressing his hand against my body.

"If the two of you could stop pawing each other," said Rosa, "I'd really like to know who thinks I'm hot."

But just then we saw Nicole waving and coming toward us. "Hi, Carlos." She leaned over and kissed the top of his head. His shirt was open, and her beaded dreadlocks brushed against his chest. He put his free arm around her and squeezed. I felt the lurch in my stomach. Was this what jealousy felt like? I guess so because I wanted to push Nicole away.

Nicole sat down. "The notice is up already," she told us.

"What notice?" asked Rosa.

"The one for the dance workshop. We do one every year in October. It's a show for the school. All the dance classes do something. DansCool does a few numbers and . . . "

I guess she saw my look because she went on in a hurry. "No wait. Don't get upset. Just listen. Every dancer can make up a number and audition to get in the show. Lee, this is your chance."

I stared at her.

"So you didn't make the company. Now you can show everyone what you can do anyway," Nicole explained. "And besides, you should have heard the older girls after the audition. They wanted your autograph after what you did to Victoria."

"What did I do to her? She's in and I'm not."

"Yeah, well, that part's too bad. But still. You made fun of her. No one does that. And you're so much better than her. We could all see it. And you know what? She could see it too. She tried to hide it, but she didn't take her eyes off of you when you danced. So see? You've got to do something in the show. This is your chance. Do it for us!"

She was so serious I laughed. "I'll read the notice.

I'll think about it."

Carlos walked me to my next class. "Was Nicole one of your girlfriends?" I asked. I tried to sound like I didn't care, but I don't think I did a good job.

Carlos stopped walking and grabbed my arm. It hurt, but he didn't let go. "Whoa. Is that the green-eyed monster?" he asked.

I must have looked stupid.

"Envy. Shakespeare. From the play *Othello*. You know," he added.

I shook my head. "I told you I don't know Shakespeare. But yeah, envy, yeah, maybe."

Carlos pulled me to him. "I told you I like girls. And right now, I like you." He kissed my hair. I felt my body relaxing into his, just for a moment, then he pulled away. "See you later."

I watched him run down the hall. It occurred to me that he really hadn't answered my question about Nicole.

And it also occurred to me that I was falling for him fast.

CHAPTER SEVEN

Dreaming Big

Of course, I wanted to do the workshop. I *had* to do it. It was my chance to prove myself. To really dance full out. I had never made up my own dance before, but suddenly I wanted to create my own dance — a dance that was really mine.

Madame Wolfson was pleased when I told her. "This is excellent. I will choose a group of girls for you to work with."

I must have looked stunned. "Group? Oh, no, Madame Wolfson. I can't do a group. I just want to do a solo. Just for me."

"I'm afraid not. It is important that I see how you work with others, how you use space with a group. With a solo, how would I know you're not making it up on the spot?"

"But . . . but I've never done anything like this before. I can't . . . "

She interrupted me. "You have been dancing for over ten years, Lee. It is time for you to try new things." Then she smiled at me. "Do not worry so much, child. This is a safe place for you to take flight, to learn and grow."

Yeah. Take flight and crash down to earth. With everybody watching.

"I think I will give you a small group of six dancers. Not too many, you see, but enough for me to judge your ability. Come and speak to me when you have a piece of music in mind. Or would you prefer that I assign you one?"

"No!" I shouted. "I mean . . . it's all right. I'll pick something." I was afraid I might be insulting her. "I mean, shouldn't my choice of music be part of what you judge?"

"Hmmm." Madame Wolfson narrowed her eyes and looked at me. "We shall see. I will need to approve your selection, of course. But I do not expect you to use a classical piece of music, if that is what you are worrying about."

I escaped from the dance studio into the hallway. Then I walked as casually as I could into the music wing and looked around for Carlos.

I saw him, surrounded by some older girls. He had his arms around one of them.

I tried to get out before he saw me.

"Hey! *Cara mia!* Come here!" he called.

I couldn't pretend I didn't hear Carlos, so I walked over. I didn't look at him. I didn't ever want to look at him again.

"Meet my backup singers," he said.

One of the girls smacked his head. "Backup, my butt," she said. She turned to me. "*We're* the talent. We just let Carlos hang out with us. Keeps this guy

out of trouble."

"Yeah," said another girl. "That way we know where his hands are."

Everyone laughed except me. I felt stupid. Just how many girls was Carlos playing around with?

Then Carlos started playing something on the piano and all the girls started singing. I sat down and listened. They were really good. Suddenly I wished I could sing and be part of this group. I wanted to forget about my dance group and be here with them.

They finished their song and I clapped. They all smiled and said thanks and then they picked up their bags and headed out. But not before they all hugged Carlos. Were they coming on to him? Or did they just like him as a friend?

I looked up to see Carlos watching me. I went over to him and rumpled his hair.

Carlos pulled me down onto his lap and kissed me on the nose.

Then I told him about Madame Wolfson and my

group. Carlos listened to all my complaining, but when I finished, he was silent. He started fiddling with the piano, playing something tuneless. Like he was ignoring me.

But then he suddenly turned and said he had an idea.

"I've been working on this song. I was kind of wondering what to do with it. Do you want to hear it?"

"Well, yeah, I guess." What did this have to do with my dance group?

Carlos turned to the piano and started playing. The music was really frantic, angry music at first, and then it got really quiet. It started to build up to something, then stopped and went all soft. And it did this, back and forth, back and forth, until it ended with a really upbeat bit, the kind of stuff that makes you feel like you want to skip around like a little kid.

He finished and turned around.

"It's great. Really great," I said. "You wrote it?"

Carlos nodded. "I was thinking about doing it for music night."

"You should. It sounds really . . . professional."

He smiled. "But here's my idea. How about if you used it for a dance?"

I guess I just stared.

"It could be really neat. Really different."

Yeah, really different. Weird.

"What do you think?" he asked.

"Well . . . I was thinking . . . don't get me wrong. I love your music. But I was thinking of using hip hop or something lyrical or . . . . "

"Oh sure. That's what everybody does here." Carlos said with a frown. "Fine. It doesn't matter. If the music doesn't work, it doesn't work. You're in charge."

You're in charge.

I heard the words for the first time. I felt a shiver up my spine. But not from fear, like when Madame Wolfson stuck me with this gig. I thought of Carlos writing music and those girls singing and suddenly

I wanted to be like them. Big. Bigger than what I was used to. Dream big. That was it.

"Do you have a CD?" I asked. "Can you burn me a copy?"

Carlos jumped up and down and did a little kid's happy dance. "You'll do it? Really?"

"Down, boy. I just want to listen to it a few times. Think it over. At home. By myself. Not with you drooling all over me like a lost puppy."

Carlos started whimpering, and then he started licking my face like he was a dog. I smelled his breath, all minty from gum. I sat still and closed my eyes. *Please*, I thought. *Please kiss me*. And he did. But this time it was more than just a brush on the lips. I thought my knees were going to give out. Then I kissed him back. Hard.

"Hey!" he said, pulling back. "Not like that. Let your lips go soft. Like this."

I felt his tongue brush my lips and I tried to relax. Then his lips were on mine and they were like something melting.

"That's right," he whispered. "Soft, like you." And then I felt his hands running up and under my sweater.

I pulled back, confused.

He sat back. "What is it?" he asked. "I thought you liked me."

"I do. I do like you. Just . . ." I didn't know what to say.

Carlos hugged me again. "Come on, Lee. You're in high school now."

I tightened my arms around him. "Just give me a bit more time. Okay?"

Carlos shrugged. He handed me his CD. "Don't make me wait too long. I really need you."

I didn't want to wait, either. I needed him, too. But I was scared.

For the next few nights, I listened to the CD over and over again. It was my treat for getting through English and history homework. I fell asleep thinking about Carlos, feeling his kiss, thinking about his hands, his perfect hands on my body. I didn't know how I could use the song, but I wanted to listen to it. I went to bed early every night, just so I could be alone with Carlos.

Rosa teased me about Carlos every day, but she was okay with it. It was Nicole who surprised me. One day, she saw me coming out of the music room and caught up to me. We talked a bit and then she said, "You really like Carlos. But be careful, Lee. He's a player."

"What are you talking about?" I asked.

"Look. He's really nice," Nicole answered. "He's a sweetheart. Last year all the girls wanted to be with him. He just ... understands girls, you know? But he plays around. It's fun to tease, but don't depend on him, that's all."

"You're crazy. I *know* he likes girls. But he's not just playing with me. We really work, okay?"

And then I figured it out. Boy, was I stupid.

"Wait a minute," I said. "You're just warning me off Carlos, aren't you? You're jealous of us, right?"

Nicole got this look on her face. "Get a grip, Lee."

"No way. Just forget about it. This year, it's me and Carlos," I said.

Nicole shook her head. "You really are a newbie, aren't you?" She turned and walked off.

I was mad. And I was sure I was right. But Nicole didn't know about Carlos's CD. She didn't know I was going to use it for my dance. Carlos and I were a partnership. We were special. Maybe Carlos did play a lot. But not with me. With me it was real. I didn't have to worry about Nicole. Carlos was mine now.

It was about a week later when Madame Wolfson asked me to come by the DansCool rehearsal. When I got there, they were working on a song by Nine Inch Nails. A very strong, street-style number. I was shocked that the Wolf had picked this kind of music.

Madame Wolfson told me to sit down and watch. She made them go over and over the same few counts several times. They were pretty good, and I felt stupid again. I could have been up there.

Finally she called for a break. And when all the others had their water bottles and towels, Madame Wolfson introduced me. I saw Julie and Victoria smirk.

"I have asked Lee to create a number for a small group. I have chosen six of you to work with her. Please understand that this will count for marks and I expect you all to give Lee your very best." Then Madame Wolfson glanced at a paper and read off six names. Aaron, Jamal, Nicole, Azama, Rosa and — surprise, surprise — Victoria. Rosa cheered. Nicole wouldn't look at me. Azama gave me a thumbs up. And Victoria looked like she'd eaten something really bad.

"I don't think so," she said.

"I beg your pardon?" asked Madame Wolfson.

"I said, I don't want to work with an amateur."

Good! Oh, please, Madame Wolfson, get rid of her!

But no.

"Victoria. I placed you in this group for a reason.

I want you to gain experience working with young dancers. It is easy to perform well when you're guided by the hand of experience. But if you have any plans at all of having a dance career, you must learn how to work with all sorts of people."

"Of course, Madame Wolfson," said Victoria. "But when will I ever have to work with trailer trash?"

The cane came crashing down on the piano bench.

"I will not tolerate such rudeness," declared Madame Wolfson. "One more comment like that and I will ask you to leave our company. Do you understand, Victoria?"

Victoria looked at Madame Wolfson. She didn't seem worried at all. Then she looked at me. "Yes, Madame Wolfson."

But to me she mouthed, "Bitch."

My face burned. I hated her. Hated her!

That night I listened to Carlos's CD again. But for the first time I didn't think about him sitting at the piano. I didn't think about his gorgeous hands and his dark brown eyes and his long, curly hair. I didn't think about kissing him. Instead I thought about that first day, crossing over Division Street. Was I glad? Did I do the right thing?

The music got loud and soft, loud and soft, back and forth, back and forth, finally reaching that wonderful happy ending.

And suddenly I sat up in bed. It was me. The music. It was my story. It was me deciding to cross Division. It was me struggling back and forth, back and forth. I got why Madame Wolfson kept talking about my story.

And I wondered — would I ever get to the happy ending?

CHAPTER EIGHT

Betrayal

The next day, Madame Wolfson left me alone with my group. This was it. This was the big test. If I couldn't pull this off, I might as well leave the school for good.

I played the music. No one said anything, and I played it again.

"I thought about doing hip hop," I said, "but then Carlos gave me this. He wrote it. I played it over and over and I finally figured out it was about struggle. It was about breaking through to a better place. It made me think of what I'm going through, coming to a new school. But I think it's about what all dancers go through. Pushing ourselves to break through to the next level."

"It's boring," said Victoria.

"Oh shut up, Vicky," said Azama. "Lee's idea sounds really different." She looked at me. "I'm glad we're not doing more hip hop, but how are you going to work this out?"

So I told them my concept. There would be an imaginary line across the center of the stage and we would be always trying to push through it. We'd dance up to it and struggle with it. But our dancing wouldn't be great. We'd pull our leaps and stumble here and there. But finally, one by one, we'd cross over. The happy ending would be all of us together, dancing full out at the front of the stage. We'd finally be dancing our best and reaching out to the audience.

"I'm calling it 'Breakthrough,'" I said.

"Let me get this straight." It was Victoria. "We're

the best dancers in the school and we have to stumble? Are you stupid? Well . . . yes, you are, aren't you?"

I went red. I couldn't speak.

"I like it." It was Jamal. "It's contemporary stuff. Like Alvin Ailey or Danny Grossman. It tells a story."

And for the first time, since that day, Nicole spoke to me. "It sounds cool. Not like that cheesy competition crap."

I smiled. Then I said, "But I need to have one dancer who really has to struggle harder than the others." I turned to Victoria. "I'd like you to do it."

I wanted to find a way to make peace with Victoria. I wanted to keep her happy and onside.

She didn't take it that way. "So you've made me the dummy? I get to look worse than the others?"

"No. Your struggle is harder, and that makes you the center of attention. I'm giving you the lead part," I told her.

"Victoria," said Azama. "Get over yourself, okay?"

"Fine," Victoria said. But I didn't like the way she looked at me.

And so, finally, we started working. Three days a week, I had studio space and my group for about an hour. I made a mess of things a few times, and I had to redo a chunk that just wasn't working. And then, after two weeks, I knew I had made a big mistake. Victoria couldn't do the steps. Whenever she had to stumble or fall, she looked sloppy. If I wanted her to look tired and worn out, she just looked bored.

I finally snapped. "Victoria! You look like overcooked spaghetti. I need some body tension. You have to fall with poise. With grace!"

She gave me the finger and walked off the stage.

But she was back the next day.

Azama pulled me aside. "You should have heard the balling out she got from Madame Wolfson," she whispered to me. "Said she couldn't stand you and refused to come back. But the Wolf really let her have it. We couldn't hear everything because she shut her office door. But we all knew Vicky was crying. She looked like hell."

Oh, great. Now I get to deal with all her crap.

And sure enough, she glared at me at every rehearsal. And I didn't like the way she watched me whenever Carlos came by. He'd come over and touch me or give me a hug. Once he let out a big whoop in the middle of the dance. "This is great! I love it! Love it!" Then he grabbed me and kissed me in front of everyone. Sometimes, I looked over at Nicole, to see how she was taking this. She never met my eyes. But she didn't give me any attitude. She just wasn't my friend anymore.

I did something else with my dance. After the first rehearsal, it wasn't hard to figure out which grade ten boy had the hots for Rosa. Jamal couldn't take his eyes off her. And Rosa? She managed to always be near him, brushing up against him. So I made up a partnering bit. Once the dancers had broken through the barrier, I had Rosa leap into Jamal's arms. He did a great lift, tossed her into the air and then caught her again. Then they held hands for the last few seconds of the piece.

Rosa finally figured out I'd done her a favor. "I'm crazy about him," she gushed. "And now we get to touch all the time. I love you!" But then she got quiet. "You know I can't bring him home. I can't tell my parents. My dad would kill me."

Jamal was listening. "You think my mom would be thrilled I want to be with a whitey? I'll be in just as much crap as you."

Carlos's reaction was typical. "Oh wow! It's *Romeo and Juliet*! They weren't allowed to fall in love. Shakespeare, you know."

"Yes, I do know," I shot back. "I've seen the ballet three times, so there!"

"Well, we're not planning on dying," declared Rosa. "Just having some fun. Come on, Jamal. Let's practice our lift."

Oh, right. She should have said, "practice our touching."

But I was no better. I couldn't wait to see Carlos after school each day. If he wasn't in the studio with me, I'd go find him in the music room. I had to be with him. I was going crazy wanting to kiss him. I'd finally told my mom about him. We'd gone to a couple of parties together and I didn't want her to worry about me being out alone. But my mom did worry. "Just be careful, Lee," she said.

"But I'll be with Carlos. I'll be fine."

"It's Carlos I'm worried about. He's your first boyfriend. Be careful, baby."

"Oh Mom! It's not like that!"

But it sure was. I knew just what my mom was talking about. And if she could see me, sitting in Carlos's lap, dancing close, stopping to kiss every two minutes . . . well . . . we'd have to have "the talk" again.

"When do I get to meet him?" she asked.

"Tomorrow. He'll be at the dance workshop."

Tomorrow.

I couldn't believe it. Were we ready? We *weren't* ready.

I dumped my cereal bowl in the sink. "I've got to

go," I told my mom. "Today's the last rehearsal. I'll be late tonight."

After school I ran to the studio. "Tomorrow's the show," I reminded everyone. "Let's do 'Breakthrough' full out this time."

Everyone put their heart into it. Even Victoria. At the end of the piece, Victoria was left alone on stage, in the spotlight. She twirled around, big smile, arms wide open to welcome her new beginning.

We all clapped for her.

Afterward, I saw her in the dressing room. She was brushing out her hair and it hung down to her waist. It was blonde — the real thing. I noticed her Rock and Republic jeans and her Diesel heels. And she had one of the big Coach bags. She had it all. But today, for once, it didn't bother me. I had my show tomorrow. And I had Carlos. Things were pretty good, I told myself.

Victoria saw me in the mirror and smiled at me. "I'm really looking forward to tomorrow," she said. "It will be so exciting for you. What you've worked so hard for. You deserve everything that happens."

I was really surprised, but I smiled back. "Thanks, Victoria. I'm, uh, glad we got to work together. And . . ." I wondered if I should say it, but I blurted it out, "I've always wanted to apologize to you. About the audition. I was rude and childish and . . . well . . . I'm glad you're here, that's all."

She smiled again, then linked arms with me. "Come on, Lee. Let's see what Carlos is up to."

We walked down the hall to the music room. Victoria quietly pulled open the door and I walked through.

A girl was sitting in Carlos's lap.

They didn't see us, because they were making out. Making out!

My eyes blurred and my heart stopped. It stopped. I could barely breathe, but I found the strength to turn and run.

Victoria was still holding the door open.

And she was laughing.

CHAPTER NINE

The Truth

I don't know how I got out of that room and down the hall to my locker. I can't remember leaving the school. But I do remember running across Division Street without pushing the crosswalk signal. And again I heard the screech of tires. Just hit me, I thought. Get this stupid thing over with.

I told my mom I was too nervous to eat dinner. I told my mom I had a ton of homework and went to my room. The phone rang a million times but I said I didn't want to talk to anybody.

"But it's Carlos. He calls every two minutes," my mom said.

"I don't want to talk to him!" I shouted.

Then Rosa started calling. I couldn't talk to her, either. I didn't want to know if she'd heard what happened. I didn't want to know what people were saying about me.

I didn't listen to Carlos's music that night. I couldn't, because I scratched his CD with scissors and threw it in the garbage.

I didn't sleep. I cried. And in the morning I lied to my mom and told her I had a late start because of the workshop after school.

"I'll see you there, baby. You'll be wonderful," my mom said.

So she left for work and I took the phone off the hook. I got back in bed and finally fell asleep.

I woke up at lunchtime because someone was pounding on the door. I pulled back the curtain and then let it drop.

"Go away," I shouted to Nicole.

"Let me in, Lee," Nicole shouted back. "I'm going to stand here and shout till you do."

I ignored her, but then she started singing that stupid kids' song "The Ants Go Marching In."

I opened the door.

"Why are you here? To gloat?" I asked.

She pushed past me and sat down. "You were wrong that day. I'm not jealous of you. I never wanted to go out with Carlos. I told you. He's a player. He's fun, Lee, and lots of girls like playing around with him. But that's all."

What was I supposed to say?

Nicole sighed. "Look. I'm sorry. You really do like Carlos. I should have kept my mouth shut."

"Why?" I asked her. "Turns out, you were right. He's a jerk."

"Well . . . I shouldn't have called you a 'newbie.' But you were just so prissy about it. All true love crap. You got on my nerves," Nicole said.

I sat down. "It doesn't matter now, does it? Does everybody know? Did Victoria tell everyone?"

"Yeah, she did. But no one cares. She's poison and everyone knows it," Nicole replied. Then she stood up. "Listen. You've had all night and most of the morning to feel sorry for yourself. Now come back to school. You can't let that bitch ruin your dance. And you can't let Carlos get away with this."

I didn't say anything.

"Come on, Lee. What about us? We want to do 'Breakthrough.' Don't you want to see your piece performed?"

I guess that's what did it. I didn't want to see Victoria or Carlos ever again. But I did want to see my dance done at least once.

Nicole waited till I showered and got ready.

I tried to get into school without anyone seeing me. I had phoned in sick in the morning. I didn't need to go to any classes. I could just show up at the assembly.

But of course, as I snuck by the dance studio, Madame Wolfson opened the door. She grabbed my arm and pulled me inside.

"So! Some boy jilts you and you forget about your art? You forget all about the dance? And you think that you are a dancer? An artist?"

I tried to say something but she kept on.

"You are young, and, yes, you are foolish. You will make many mistakes in love and in life. But Lee — and I want you to hear this, so listen — dance always comes first. Dance must own you. Dance makes the rules. Not some boy. Not anyone. Only you. Only your art can tell you what to do."

I nodded. I knew that I could not give up dance because of my dad or Victoria or Carlos.

"Good!" said Madame Wolfson. "Now I want to see you with your head held high." Then she cupped my face in her hands. "You have a gift, Lee. You must not throw it away."

On my way to the dressing room, Rosa ran up and hugged me.

"I know what Victoria did," Rosa said. "I grabbed Carlos this morning and almost killed him."

"What do you mean, 'what Victoria did'? She

didn't do anything. Other than laugh at me."

"She set you up," Rosa said. "That girl Carlos was with is her cousin. Carlos went out with her a few times last year. Victoria got her here on purpose. I told you, she set you up."

I staggered and reached out a hand to a locker. Relief flooded through my body! Carlos was. . . .

Carlos was a jerk. I saw him pawing a girl. Didn't matter if she was his ex.

A minute later, I saw Carlos coming down the hall. He stopped when he saw me.

"Hi, Lee." He looked at Rosa. "Can I talk to Lee alone?"

"Nope," said Rosa. She put her hands on her hips. That settled it, as far as she was concerned.

I just couldn't help it. I started to laugh. But I stopped when I saw the dirty look Carlos gave Rosa.

"We'll talk later," I told him. "But right now, I need a CD of your music. There's something wrong with mine."

"Sure. I'll bring it to the studio," Carlos said. He

turned and walked off.

"Do NOT take him back!" Rosa threatened.

But then Madame Wolfson swooped down on us. "Girls, girls, into the change room."

The show began with a jazz routine by DansCool. I watched from backstage and had to admit they were good. Hard to believe the audition was only six weeks ago.

Then the grade nines were up with our class ballet number. I put everything into it. I had to — this was all the dancing I got to do today.

As soon as we were finished, I changed clothes. Madame Wolfson said I'd be called out for a bow after my piece, and I wanted to look perfect. It had taken a bit of time, but Rosa and I had fun combing the second hand stores for the right look. I ended up with skinny black jeans and a sort of tuxedo look black satin jacket.

"Very New York," said Rosa.

'Breakthrough' was the last number of the show, so I could watch some of the other dances. Halfway through, I went to the studio to get ready. Carlos was waiting for me outside the door.

"Here's the CD," he said.

"Thanks." I put my hand on the doorknob.

"Lee. I'm sorry you're upset. But come on. It was just a kiss."

"It was a lot more than a kiss," I said. "But maybe it was my fault. I know you like girls. You told me all the time you like girls. I just was hoping . . . I guess that you liked me best."

"I do. You have this amazing talent. I want to do a solo piece for you. I've started already." Carlos reached for my hand. "Give me another chance."

I didn't let him touch me. "I have to get everyone ready."

"Sure. 'Breakthrough' is going to be great. Your routine. My music. We make a great team. I mean it." He moved his body in close. "Come on, Lee. Let me prove it to you."

I felt myself tense up, and I moved back. "Got to go," I said.

But Carlos grabbed my hand. "Why so frigid?" he asked. "I mean, maybe if you put out a bit more I wouldn't need anyone else."

What a jerk. What a huge, capital letters JERK.

"Let go," I said, and I jerked my hand away.

I walked into the studio and sat down. I was shaking.

"You all right?" Nicole asked.

I took a deep breath. "I will be."

Then, one by one the other dancers came in and got into the costume for my number. We had decided to keep it simple. The girls wore black leotards and shorts, bare legs. Jamal and Aaron had black tanks and jazz pants.

"Where's Victoria?" I asked.

"She's doing her last number," explained Azama.

But just then, Julie pushed the door open. Victoria hobbled in, supported by two student stagehands. She was crying and moaning.

"It's her ankle!" cried Julie. "She sprained it."

Someone ran for Madame Wolfson. Someone

else got some ice.

"I did not see you hurt yourself, Victoria," Madame Wolfson said. "When did this happen?"

"Just when she came offstage," answered Julie. She was hurrying for Lee's thing and she just . . . fell."

"I see. Thank goodness that you made it through the rest of the show before this . . . accident."

There was something in Madame Wolfson's voice that made me look at her.

"I'm so sorry, Lee," Victoria whispered. "I really am."

And there was something in her voice that made me look at her, too.

Madame Wolfson turned to me. "What will you do?"

I was confused. "Do? We'll . . . we'll have to cancel. We can't do the number without Victoria."

"Nonsense!" replied Madame Wolfson. "You can't let this happen. In the real world, a show doesn't stop just because someone is hurt. An understudy steps in. The routine is changed. Now then, what will you do?"

I couldn't believe this! What was I supposed to do? And why me? What did I do to deserve all this crap?

"You have about fifteen minutes, Lee," Madame Wolfson said.

"It's easy, Madame Wolfson," Nicole said. "Lee will do Victoria's part."

What?!

"Perfect," agreed Madame Wolfson.

"No! No, I can't!"

"Someone run to Lee's locker," demanded Azama. "We need her black leotard and shorts. Hurry! She's going to dance!"

CHAPTER TEN

Breakthrough

I ran into the change room. Could I do this? Could I? I closed my eyes. Don't cry! Don't! I knew the dance. It was *my* dance. But I hadn't rehearsed with the others. Could I pull this off?

Rosa followed me in. "You can do this, *cara mia*," said Rosa. "It's your story, remember?"

I turned to Rosa and smiled. "What the hell," I said. "What else could go wrong?"

I stood backstage, waiting for my part. And I remembered my old teacher telling me not to

compete. Just dance.

Just.

Dance.

That's what I did. I heard the music and I felt the struggle. I danced for myself. I danced for everyone who tries so hard. And at the end, when the spotlight was trained on me, I opened my arms wide to the audience, inviting them into my story.

The applause was wild. People stood up and cheered. I felt like a zombie. I bowed and smiled and thought I'd faint. I finally got off the stage, but then Carlos and I were brought back and introduced.

Carlos took my hand and kissed it.

Oh yeah?

I put my arms around him and kissed him on the lips. Just like the dance, I gave it everything I had. Then I let go of him and walked off stage.

I didn't look back.

Ciuco.

*   *   *

So much happened after that. People were all around me, telling me how much they liked the show. My mom hugged me and couldn't stop crying.

Then Madame Wolfson waved me over.

"Lee, this is Mr. Wyatt," she told me. "He is the manager of the local television station, CBKT. He'd like to speak to you."

I smiled at Mr. Wyatt.

"We have an upcoming charitable event, and we want to showcase some local talent. I'd like to offer your dancers a spot on the show. Interested?"

"Oh! Oh, yes! Oh, Mr. Wyatt! Thank you!"

"I'll interview you about 'Breakthrough' before the show, and then we'll tape the dance. Here's my card. Call tomorrow to set it up."

I thanked him again.

I wanted to tell the others right away, but Madame Wolfson put her arm around me.

"I am very proud of you, Lee. You have shown me that I was right about you."

I nodded. "Thank you, Madame Wolfson." I looked at Mr. Wyatt's card. "This would never have happened if it wasn't for you."

She smiled at me. "By the way, I think that Victoria's . . . injury will keep her from participating. You will have to perform her part on television. In fact, I will have to insist that Victoria not take part in DansCool for the next few months. I wouldn't want her ankle to get any worse. I expect to see you at rehearsal tomorrow."

So that was that. I was finally in DansCool.

This time, I deserved it.

One final thing. We all went back to Carlos's house. His dad had ordered in lots of food and we had a great time.

Then this guy in grade eleven asked me if I'd like to go out with him sometime.

"Maybe go to a movie?"

"Sure," I said. "That'd be fun."

I had finally figured out dance.

Now I wanted to figure out boys.